The Secret Elephants

THE
SECRET
ELEPHANTS

by Catharine Marsden

ILLUSTRATED BY LILIAN OBLIGADO

New York

E.P. DUTTON & CO., INC.

TO

Sister Alma Maria

Contents

The Secret Elephants

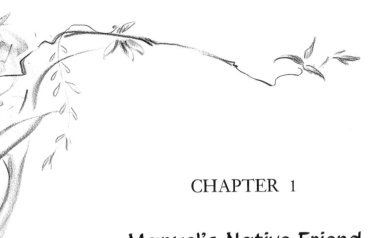

CHAPTER 1

Manuel's Native Friend

Mozambique is in southeastern Africa. The Portuguese settled there hundreds of years ago. They found the land fertile and beautiful, the rivers deep, and the veldt endless. So they made friends with the natives, built trading posts and towns, and lived happily and productively.

Manuel Lopez, a Portuguese boy, lived in Mozambique. He was home now on vacation from his school in Johannesburg. He sat on the veranda of his father's trading post, watching his brown lizard sunning himself. The lizard was covered with pointed warts, and was puffed out from eating all the insects that Manuel caught for it.

Manuel wondered why Bolamba, his native friend, did not come out of the veldt to see him. Surely Bolamba knew that school was out. Manuel stretched lazily. Like the lizard, he was enjoying the sun.

His father, Carlos Lopez, was inside the trading post talking to Mr. Hammar, a German hunter, who was buying equipment for another safari into the jungle.

"Give me more ammunition, and several good lanterns." The cold, rasping voice of the hunter pierced the air. It made Manuel shudder. Yet his father answered Mr. Hammar politely and in a gentle voice.

"Fill the truck with gasoline and put oil in the drums," ordered Mr. Hammar.

"Yes, sir," said Carlos softly. "And do you need any khaki shirts?"

"Not those," sneered the hunter, fingering the shirts spread out on a table. "I wouldn't be caught dead in those."

"Perhaps you would like some canned soups," persisted Carlos. Manuel grinned as he listened. He knew that his quiet father would be a match for the hunter, and make a profit, too, so that Manuel could continue his education in Johannesburg.

His pet lizard was now doing push-ups, probably hoping to impress a female lizard. Manuel tossed him a dead beetle, and looked out over the veldt.

He wondered if Mr. Hammar would be hunting lions. Most European hunters did . . . big showy lions that could be photographed and exhibited back home. Mozambique was famous for these tawny creatures, as well as zebras, leopards, baboons, wart hogs, and elephants.

But because of the nearby Kosa tribe, no one hunted the elephants. These native Africans believed that the spirits of their brave warriors lived again in the elephants, the Sacred Elephants. So no one killed them.

Manuel's mother, Maria, taught a class of African children in the mission school. It was she who had first told Manuel: "Respect the elephants. They never come near our trading post or kraals. They do us no harm, and the Kosas honor them."

Manuel's father sold no equipment for elephant hunting, and he did not send native guides out after the animals. At the nearby Forestry Station, the officials gave no permits to hunt elephants.

Mr. Hammar was asking about elephants now. The foreign hunters were always asking about elephants.

"Why can't I get a permit to hunt elephants?" questioned the German.

"The Forestry Station will not give a permit to hunt them," explained Carlos. "Lions, yes—but elephants, no."

"Why? Why?" barked the hunter. He knows why, thought Manuel contemptuously. He is just giving Father a hard time.

"It is because of the nearby Kosa tribe," explained Carlos. How patient Father is! thought Manuel.

"These native Africans believe that the spirits of their

13

brave warriors live again in the elephants," Carlos told Mr. Hammar. "Therefore the elephants are sacred. No one hunts them."

Mr. Hammar cursed under his breath, took his purchases, and departed.

Father is really a wonderful man, Manuel thought. In addition to catering to the hunters and supplying their needs, he traded clothes, groceries, medicine, and candy to the natives for corn, peanuts, animal skins, and small game. Yes, thought Manuel, his father's trading post was very useful to the hunters and the natives.

Manuel watched his lizard bowing to the floor in front of an ordinary-looking female lizard that had suddenly appeared. The female seemed to pay no attention to the male at first. Then suddenly they both darted into the grass.

Manuel chuckled. He looked past the grass and flowering trees. Why didn't Bolamba come? He must know that Manuel was home from school. In some mysterious way the natives knew everything the white people did.

Then suddenly Bolamba appeared on the veranda. Manuel had not heard his soft footsteps.

"So you've come at last. I'm glad to see you," said Manuel, grinning at the tall ebony-colored boy. "I've been saving some lemonade for you."

Bolamba was a Kosa. His father was chief of the Kosa tribe.

He was wearing a cotton shirt and pants given him by Maria,
Manuel's mother.

Mother was always wanting to cover up the nakedness of
the natives, Manuel thought to himself. But on Bolamba the
clothing looked fine.

Maria came out on the veranda and greeted Bolamba
warmly. She was little and round and smelled of spicy cooking.

"Good afternoon, Bolamba. Now, don't you look nice
in those clothes," Marie praised Bolamba. The boy's face
brightened with a pleased smile.

Manuel grinned. He knew that Bolamba discarded his clothes in the jungle and covered his body with stripes of paint, but Manuel was thankful that his friend wore clothes when he visited the trading post.

Sometimes the Lopez family heard sounds of drums and native dances in the night, but they pretended not to notice. The Kosas were friendly. Their children flocked to the mission school and learned to speak Portuguese. They joined in the songs like "God Bless Africa," shouting and clapping to the rhythm. The older natives traded at the store. They liked and respected Manuel's parents.

"What have you been doing while I was in school?" asked Manuel.

"I was gun carrier on a hunt for Simba the lion," replied Bolamba. He gulped down the lemonade Manuel had given him.

Just then Mr. Hammar returned with a great screeching of brakes, and shouted for Carlos to bring him some tobacco.

"Can you take me for a ride in your father's jeep?" Bolamba spoke softly to Manuel. "I have something wonderful to show you." The boy's dark eyes sparkled with excitement.

"Of course. Wait until I ask Father," and Manuel jumped from the veranda, ran out to his father, and asked, "Father, may we go for a ride in the jeep?"

"Yes, of course," replied Carlos. "There is some hay in the back of the jeep. Leave it in the kraals for the calves before you return, please."

Mr. Hammar was lighting his pipe. "Do you allow your son to associate with natives?" he questioned in a loud voice.

"Bolamba is a fine boy," replied Carlos. "I am proud that Manuel goes with him."

Manuel's face burned with shame at Mr. Hammar's question, but he was gratified by his father's reply.

"Which way shall I drive?" Manuel asked Bolamba as they climbed into the jeep.

"Down the elephant road," replied Bolamba quietly.

Out of the corner of his eye Manuel saw that his native friend was smiling. He also had heard Carlos's reply.

Manuel sped down the road in the jeep. He liked to ride out here on the veldt. Bolamba had often told him about this road and how, long ago, it had been an elephant path. White men had improved the road, and now it was used by cars and jeeps and trucks.

Manuel drove expertly. His father did not allow him to drive in Johannesburg, but out here it was different. Manuel was even teaching Bolamba to drive.

Manuel stepped on the gas. It was like flying over the grasses of the veldt. It was a fine change from school.

"Tomorrow you must try driving again," Manuel said to Bolamba.

"Yes, I am anxious to drive," replied Bolamba. "But the engine frightens me. It moves so suddenly when I step on the gas."

Manuel laughed. Bolamba was not joking. He really was a little afraid of the jeep.

The road now went over a small mangrove swamp, and then on to a stretch of dry land. Manuel heard the discordant sounds of monkeys in the trees, and bright birds rose in flight before them.

Once they passed a snake curled up on a stone, sunning itself.

"Snakes, that's what I'm afraid of," Manuel said. "Did you see that puff adder?"

"Yes, I saw him," answered Bolamba. "The puff adder is the most dangerous of all snakes. You must stay far away from him."

"Oh, don't worry, I will. I am afraid of all of them," exclaimed Manuel. "I am afraid of the cobras, full of poison and ready to spit in your face. And I'm afraid of the mambas, too. They rise up high on their tails and leer at you before striking. I saw one strike a calf last year." Manuel shivered. The poor little calf had swelled up and died.

The boys came to an expanse of land covered with matted spears of sisal.

"There are many snakes in the sisal," Bolamba said, and then he laughed as Manuel shivered again.

"Never do anything to frighten a snake, if you are so afraid of them," advised Bolamba. "A snake attacks only if you frighten it. Always remember that."

"Oh, I will," promised Manuel.

On and on the jeep bounced. They passed red and yellow poinsettias and giant begonias. Mother would like to see these, Manuel thought. He would bring her out some day.

"How much farther do we have to go?" he asked Bolamba. "What is it that you're going to show me?"

"We are going to the high bluff this side of the deep river," Bolamba said, and pointed to the towering hill in the distance.

"What are we going to see there?" Manuel insisted. He had seen the river often.

"The Sacred Elephants," Bolamba replied solemnly. "The Sacred Elephants have returned from the far country. There is a herd now down in the river under the bluff."

"Elephants!" Manuel stepped on the gas. "How wonderful!"

"But we must stop now and climb up the bluff quietly." Bolamba motioned for Manuel to stop the jeep. "The elephants might hear us."

CHAPTER 2

The Sacred Elephants

Elephants! Sacred Elephants! Manuel was jubilant. Never before had he seen such a wonderful sight.

There they were, down on the riverbank, the herd of mighty animals. The big gray wrinkled bull elephant in the water appeared to be the leader. He was hosing down his skin. His ears were like sails, and his legs like strong columns. And what a trunk! It was as big as Manuel's whole body.

"See the bull elephant's eyes." Manuel spoke softly. The boys were stretched out on the matted grass, looking down at the herd in the river. The eyes of the old bull were amber-colored and set in the sides of his monstrous head.

There were the cow elephants, looking sideways at their children.

"Elephants cannot see straight ahead because their faces are too wide, and so their eyes are set on the sides of their heads," Bolamba told Manuel.

"This is wonderful," whispered Manuel.

They watched the baby elephants too, stamping and splashing in the water. Some of the mothers were washing their young ones. One baby curled his trunk back out of the way and nursed from the two breasts hanging down between his mother's front legs. First he nursed one breast, and then the other.

"What a greedy little fellow!" said Manuel. He drew a deep breath and surveyed the scene below. "I am so glad you brought me to see this."

White egrets moved among the elephants, catching mosquitoes and other insects.

"Sometimes mosquitoes get into the wrinkled skin of the elephants and almost drive them crazy," Bolamba explained. "The birds are a help to the elephants."

Manuel peered through the sisal intently. An enormous elephant below seemed to be on guard. He would lift his sensitive trunk into the air, as if testing, and then trumpet loudly.

And the whole herd made noises in their throats and stomachs, creating a loud rumbling of sounds.

As the wind blew the strong odor of the elephants toward Manuel, he realized that he and Bolamba were safe from discovery by the old elephant on guard.

"Come," said Bolamba, "I have more to show you around the bend in the river," and he led Manuel away. The boys circled another bluff and looked down on the river again.

"Wart hogs! Big ugly wart hogs!" exclaimed Manuel, amazed. There were so many of them.

The wart hogs were like great blobs of mud in the river. Their protruding eyes stuck out above the water. They snorted and sloshed and made loud sucking noises. It was a wild sight. More wart hogs were wallowing on the muddy bank of the river . . . wart hogs with hairless bodies, long warts, and dangerous tusks. The young ones tumbled about their mothers, who grunted at them in grating tones.

Suddenly Manuel heard angry trumpeting from up the river.

"Let's go back. Something has happened," said Bolamba.

The loud, harsh trumpeting filled the jungle. When they returned to the top of the first bluff, Manuel saw the bull elephant again. He stood tall, his trunk aloft, calling his herd out of the river and into the jungle.

"Can we follow them a little way?" asked Manuel.

Bolamba shook his head. "There is no end to the jungle, and night is coming," he whispered. "No one stays out in the jungle at night. Come, we must leave the river."

Bolamba led the way back to the jeep. Just as Manuel was about to jump into the front seat, he saw the baby elephant. He was eating the hay Manuel's father had put in the jeep for the calves. How had he managed to climb that steep bluff?

"Don't move. You will frighten him, and then his mother will come," warned Bolamba.

Manuel watched the baby elephant greedily eat up the hay.

"How do you suppose he got up here?" he asked Bolamba.

"There is an elephant trail up the side of the bluff," Bolamba replied. "But it is steep, and the elephants don't use it very often."

"Shall I push the hay out and let him have it all?" Manuel whispered.

"Sh-hh! Don't move," Bolamba cautioned suddenly, and pointed to the brush. There stood a cow elephant, quietly looking at them.

23

The baby elephant lifted his sensitive little trunk as though searching the air for something. He put his trunk into Manuel's shirt pocket and took out a bag of peanuts. Manuel held his breath.

The mother elephant ambled toward them and rubbed her ear, big as a tabletop, against the jeep. She reached into the back with her trunk and picked up the hay. Then, trumpeting for her child to follow, she carried the hay into the brush. The baby elephant scrambled after her.

Manuel and Bolamba watched without speaking. When the two elephants were out of sight, Manuel drew a deep breath, and started the jeep back toward the trading post.

"We must drive fast," Bolamba said. "Dark comes quickly. Manuel, promise me you will never tell anyone you have seen the Sacred Elephants. This must be our secret."

"Yes," agreed Manuel. "This is our secret. I'll never tell. They are our secret elephants."

24

CHAPTER 3

Bolamba Drives the Jeep

The next day Manuel took Bolamba out to give him a driving lesson. Bolamba was wise in the ways of the jungle and veldt, but behind the wheel of the jeep he was a coward.

Manuel drove down the elephant road. Just over a rise in the land, he could see native children tending cattle. And all about fluttered the rhinoceros birds, with their little red bills. They were eating the ticks off the cattle.

Manuel's father kept his cattle inside the kraals, and dipped them regularly for ticks. Several times a year the natives helped Carlos fill a deep trench with water. Then Carlos poured chemicals into the water. This was such strong medicine that when the cattle were driven down the trench through the water, they came out bathed clean of ticks and other insects. Carlos had the finest cattle in Mozambique because of his care in ridding them of ticks. But nature's way

of removing the ticks from the cattle was good, too, Manuel thought, as he and Bolamba drove past the busy rhinoceros birds.

It was Bolamba's turn to drive. He got behind the wheel, his hands trembling.

"Remember, first you turn on the ignition," instructed Manuel. "No, not that. That is for the lights. Here, this key. Now, where is the clutch? Right. The brake? No! That's the gas!"

Bolamba had somehow put the jeep in reverse and suddenly backed it in a circle. The jeep stalled, with its back wheels two feet off the ground, high on an anthill.

26

Manuel shouted with laughter, but Bolamba's face was white with fright.

"Oh, Bolamba, don't be afraid," Manuel said. "Come on, try again."

Manuel found a larger anthill, and made Bolamba drive around it from all directions, turning to the right and then to the left, backing up, parking, and making sharp turns. By evening the earth around the anthill was covered with flattened ants, but Bolamba had progressed with his lesson, and Manuel was satisfied.

They returned to the trading post for dinner.

"Manuel," said Bolamba, "will you ask your father if you can come with me to the village and stay all night?"

"Does your father know that you are asking me?" inquired Manuel.

"Yes, he has promised us a feast of roast goat if you will come," replied Bolamba.

"Wow! Great!" shouted Manuel. The last time he had eaten at the village the chief's wife had prepared peanut gravy and manioc, which he had eaten politely, but roast goat he really liked.

"Yes, of course you may go," agreed Carlos. "Why don't you let Bolamba drive there? That would make his father proud."

"Oh, Father, what a smart man you are!" and Manuel laughed. "The chief will really like to see Bolamba drive."

"Then go with God, and return before dark tomorrow," said Carlos.

Manuel slipped into the back of the trading post and got out a can of peanuts.

"May we take this?" he asked his father.

"Surely," agreed Carlos.

Manuel climbed into the jeep beside Bolamba. He knew that his native friend would drive by the bluff again. There was no way of telling how long the herd of Sacred Elephants would stay there, and he wanted to see them again.

The elephant road was packed hard, and Bolamba drove straight down the middle of it. They stopped below the bluff and walked to where they could look down on the elephants in the river.

Manuel opened the can of peanuts, in case they could find the baby elephant again.

And there he was, down by the water. Manuel was sure it was the same one. He was attempting to nurse again. He's kind of big to be always nursing, Manuel thought.

Evidently the mother thought so too, for she pushed the baby away. When he persisted stubbornly his big mother spanked him soundly on his hind parts with her trunk.

The baby squealed in anger, and charged up the steep bank toward Manuel and Bolamba.

Manuel and Bolamba scarcely breathed, they were so quiet. Then the baby elephant saw them. He approached slowly, then more confidently. He seemed to remember them, or perhaps he smelled the peanuts in the can.

Manuel held out the can. The little elephant plunged his trunk into the peanuts and greedily put them in his mouth.

"This is much better than milk," Manuel said softly to the elephant child.

"That elephant is really hungry." Bolamba laughed. "Hear his belly rumble."

The boys stayed on the bluff a long time, feeding the little elephant a few peanuts at a time. When the sun began to set, they dumped half of the peanuts on the thick, matted grass and reluctantly returned to the jeep.

They headed toward the Kosa village. Many times Manuel had visited this village. Its mud huts with their peaked thatched roofs fascinated him. Only the chief's hut had a cor- rugated-iron roof.

The men and women and children who lived there were a happy tribe. They were tall and handsome, with black-satin skin and shining round eyes. They worked hard, trying to make a living out of the land around their village.

Bolamba's mother sang as she worked. There was always a baby riding snugly on her back, which she lulled to sleep with her melodies and swaying movements, as she swept the earth, planted, harvested, or pounded rice. She was one of the cleanest women in the village, stopping several times a day to bathe herself and her baby in the stream that flowed nearby. But, then, all of the Kosas bathed frequently.

Bolamba's father planted his few acres, hunted the veldt, occasionally served as a guide for the European hunters, ruled his people, and worked hard to provide for his many wives and children. The Kosas stored much of their plantain, corn, nuts, and rice in tightly woven baskets in the trees; and used underground storage places for roots and sweet potatoes.

As Bolamba drove the jeep nearer the village, the Kosas ran out to meet him. They shouted and laughed when they saw Bolamba driving.

The big chief was overcome with pride. His son was actually driving a jeep. Mjob, Bolamba's older brother, stared

31

unbelievingly. He was speechless, and Manuel could hardly keep from laughing at the look on his face.

"Manuel," Mjob said, "I am also your friend. Some day soon will you teach me to drive the jeep, please?"

"Some day soon," Manuel agreed.

As Bolamba had promised, the chief's wives served roast young goat to the boys that evening. The Kosas themselves also ate grasshoppers and lizards, alive and kicking in the pot, along with the roast goat.

Manuel and Bolamba stuffed themselves on the roast goat; later on, they bathed in the small stream. Then they went to bed in a hut with a peaked thatched roof. Mjob, Bolamba's brother, came into the hut to sleep with them.

Manuel liked Mjob. He was a big, handsomely tattooed boy, who spoke fluent Portuguese, which he had learned working as a guide. He often told Manuel stories about his people. Being an older boy, he did not come to the trading post to play, as Bolamba did. Mjob had responsibilities, and was even now saving up to buy his first wife.

"You must pay many calves and chickens or baskets of corn for a good wife," Mjob had once explained to Manuel. Manuel did not understand much about buying wives, but he liked the stories Mjob told about his tribe.

Manuel fell asleep listening to the lizards rustling in the thatched roof overhead.

CHAPTER 4

A Kosa Hunt

The next morning Manuel and Bolamba ate breakfast with the tribe. Breakfast was steamed plantain mixed with live red ants. Manuel had tried eating red ants before. They had tasted fishy and, though they were sort of crunchy, he did not like them. So now he ate bananas, with steamed rice over boiled fish.

There was an air of excitement in the village, and Manuel soon learned that all the men and boys were about to go on a hunt for a giant forest boar.

"Why go on the hunt today?" asked Manuel.

"Because the boar raided our food supplies again last night. He destroyed eight baskets of corn and all of our sweet potatoes," Mjob explained angrily.

"He is a big boar, with sharp tusks and black hair. He is a demon," said the chief, his dark eyes sparkling with hatred.

The chief gave Manuel a spear, somewhat smaller than the one Mjob carried.

"You may go with us," he said grandly.

Manuel gulped and almost choked on his rice. He—go on a boar hunt!

"This boar lives mostly in the bamboo forest," said Mjob. "He is very dangerous. Men hunt him. Boys follow and learn, for some day the boys will be the hunters."

Manuel felt that he was brave enough to follow and watch and learn.

The warriors came out, carrying their sharp spears high.

They chanted a song in harsh voices. Manuel knew that it

was the hunters' prayer to their gods asking that their weapons be blessed.

Mjob grabbed his spear and joined the hunters in their chant. Bolamba and Manuel held their spears high, but they did not know the words of the song.

Manuel followed the warriors into the jungle. He knew he was being greatly honored by the Kosas. After all, no other Portuguese boy had ever been taken on a hunt.

Bolamba told Manuel more about the giant boar as they followed the animal's trail. This boar ate roots, for the most part. He was magnificently ugly and cruel. He killed for the pleasure of killing.

The hunt lasted for hours, through dense jungles and matted sisal. Once the boys stopped to eat bananas, but the rest of the time they pushed onward, trying to keep in sight of the men.

Manuel often plunged his spear into the brush, trying to learn how to handle it. The end was sharp and dangerous, but he could not imagine himself having the strength to kill a giant boar with it. His father's gun would work better.

Manuel was almost exhausted with weariness when he heard shouts ahead.

"The boar is trapped," announced Bolamba with joy.

They arrived at the scene just before the boar was killed.

The beast had taken refuge in a bamboo thicket, which was now hemmed in by warriors. He was all black, bristly, and foul smelling.

The hunters killed the boar and then danced around him, chanting, stamping the ground, and shaking their spears to heaven. In this way they expressed their gratitude to their gods.

Then they made a litter of branches and dragged their prize back to the village for a celebration.

"Bolamba," Manuel said, "I cannot stay for the celebration. Father said that I must be back before dark."

The boys climbed into the jeep, waved good-by to the tribesmen, and headed for the trading post. Though they would have to hurry to get there before dark, they stopped briefly to visit the secret elephants.

They were just in time to see the huge cow elephant leading her child across the river. The little elephant held firmly to his mother's tail with his trunk, and she led him through the racing water. Manuel was delighted. The elephants were so smart—they were so much like people.

When Manuel and Bolamba finally reached the trading post, the moon was high and the sky was studded with white stars.

"We were beginning to worry about you," said Maria.

37

"Don't stay out so late again," ordered Carlos in a stern voice.

"I'm sorry that we're so late," Manuel apologized. Then he whispered to Bolamba, "May I tell them about the elephants?"

"Yes, but be sure to tell them that these are the Sacred Elephants," replied Bolamba.

After Carlos and Maria had promised that they would never reveal the secret, Manuel told them all about the elephants—about the size of the herd, the elephant families, the old guard elephant, and the baby elephant who was so friendly.

Carlos and Maria were excited over the nearness of the elephant herd.

"I hope the hunters do not hear the trumpeting," said Carlos.

Manuel and Bolamba went to bed, still excited over the frightening boar hunt and the visit to the Sacred Elephants.

Bolamba lay on a cot in Manuel's room, as he always did when he visited here. The boys stretched out under the mosquito netting and talked far into the night. Bolamba told Manuel everything he knew about elephants.

"Some of the elephants live to be a hundred years old. They have great tusks, especially the old ones, which are valuable to hunters. The elephants' legs are as large and as strong as giant trees. They have yellow eyes that cannot see far, but their keen ears can hear everything. Their long trunks, as large as a man's body, can reach up into the air and scent hunters miles away, if the wind is right. Those trunks are so sensitive, like a mother's fingers, that they can pick up a bird's egg, if they wish, without breaking the shell. And the trunks are so strong that they can hurl a man against a tree and break every bone in his body.

"The elephants feel emotions like people. They love and hate and have pride, and they grieve. Once a tribesman saw a mother elephant carrying her dead baby around with her, and the jungle shook with her cries of grief.

"The elephants are favored by the gods. No animal is bigger than they are. The whole jungle fears and respects them. The gods even send white egrets to ride on their backs and eat the insects that hide in their wrinkled, folded skin."

Early the next morning the boys were awakened by a loud knock at the door of their house. Manuel heard voices. The hunter, Mr. Hammar, was talking to Carlos.

Manuel sprang out of bed, tossing the mosquito netting aside. Bolamba sat up, and they listened through the thin partition.

"You lie to me," shouted Mr. Hammar. "I saw elephant dung on the wheels of the jeep. Your boy was on a hunt yesterday. I heard the noise of the hunters when they returned.

What did they hunt? Elephants?" The man's voice was loud with anger.

"Bring that native boy to me. Make him take me to hunt elephants. I have come a long way, and I swear I am going to hunt elephants!"

"May that hunter rot in the jungle!" swore Bolamba. "May his banana trees perish."

Carlos talked quietly to the angry man. "The boys were on a boar hunt yesterday. They did not hunt elephants. They never hunt elephants. I myself have not seen elephants around here for years." Carlos was most persuasive.

The hunter was a rude and angry man, but he finally left.

"He is going to hunt lions again," said Carlos, with a sigh of relief.

Manuel was thankful that Carlos had sent the hunter away. There must never be any hunter around the Sacred Elephants, and especially the elephant child.

CHAPTER 5

Forced Safari

The next day Carlos asked the boys to drive out to the kraals with a load of hay for the calves. Bolamba was driving with great confidence now, but as he backed the jeep around to return to the trading post, a shadow crossed the windshield.

There stood Mr. Hammar, the hunter. He held a gun in his hand, and his face was angry. His native boy guides cowered behind him.

"Take me to that elephant herd," the hunter ordered. "I know that there is one. These boy guides are so stupid. They cannot understand what I want."

They know, all right, Manuel thought. Bolamba only stared at the hunter, saying nothing.

"What elephant herd?" asked Manuel, trying to stall for time.

"Don't take me for a fool," snarled the hunter. "I heard an elephant trumpeting last night."

"But the elephants are sacred," Manuel objected. "Father said that you were going to hunt lions. . . ."

"I'll hunt elephants!" roared Mr. Hammar. "Come. Guide me to them," and he climbed into the back of the jeep.

Bolamba stepped on the gas, and the jeep plunged backward, bumping over an ant mound and making a sharp circle.

Oh, oh, thought Manuel, he's in reverse gear again.

The hunter leaped out of the jeep. "What are you trying to do?" he thundered. "Murder me? Wreck the jeep?"

"Bolamba is a new driver," explained Manuel. "I'm teaching him."

"You can't teach a native anything," shouted Mr. Hammar. "Get out, boy! You . . ." he pointed to Manuel, "get in the jeep. You drive." The big man waved his gun in Manuel's face.

Bolamba slid from behind the wheel. Quick as a flash, he climbed out of the jeep and disappeared into the veldt. As though a signal had been given, the hunter's native guides slipped away too. Only the rippling of the high grass showed where they had gone.

Manuel was frightened. Bolamba shouldn't have left him alone with the hunter. If I can only escape too, Manuel thought. But the angry hunter held the gun pressed against Manuel's ribs.

"We don't need those savages," snarled the man. "If you do not take me to the elephant herd, I will return to the trading post and shoot your father."

Manuel was terrified. The man was so ugly and belligerent. Perhaps he was mad . . . affected by the African sun. Manuel fumbled with the gear, took the car out of reverse, and started forward.

The hunter laid his gun in his lap, but his fingers were still on it. Manuel drove down the elephant road in the direction he and Bolamba had taken yesterday. Perhaps he could turn off soon and pretend that the herd was gone.

Manuel came to a good place to turn off the road, but the hunter called out in anger, "Go straight. I can see your jeep tracks. You went this way yesterday."

The man was right. The jeep tracks were plain. If the hunter had any sense, he could follow them alone.

Manuel drove on slowly. He was desperate. What could he do? He must not let the hunter get near the elephant herd.

He passed the mangrove swamp where the white egrets fed. Herons were fishing nearby. They rose with harsh screams when the jeep passed. A flock of carrion birds rose like a cloud from their feast on the body of a dead animal.

Insects swarmed around Manuel's face. Perspiration rolled down his back. He was thirsty. Though Mr. Hammar drank from his water bottle, he didn't offer to share with Manuel.

Suddenly Manuel had an inspiration. He would take the hunter to the wart hogs instead of to the Sacred Elephants. Perhaps shooting one of those ugly beasts would satisfy him.

Manuel stopped the jeep. "We must walk from here," he said, "so that the elephants will not hear us."

Mr. Hammar got out willingly enough, and Manuel led him to the second bluff, which looked down on the wart hogs.

Manuel fervently hoped that the elephant on guard wouldn't trumpet while he was showing the wart hogs to Mr. Hammar, for Manuel remembered how he and Bolamba had been able to hear the elephant trumpeting before from this very spot.

Down below the bluff the wart hogs were still huge blobs of mud on the riverbank. "Why, there are wart hogs here now," said Manuel, trying to sound surprised.

45

"Were elephants here yesterday?" asked the hunter suspiciously.

"Yesterday elephants were in the river," replied Manuel. He did not explain that they were a mile down the river.

He hoped that Mr. Hammar would kill one of the fierce wart hogs immediately. Then the noise of his shot would alarm the elephants down the river; and the big bull elephant, who was their leader, would take the herd into the jungle.

Mr. Hammar stared at the ugly beasts below, but he did not shoot. Manuel held his breath in anguish, for he thought he could hear faint elephant sounds coming from down the river bend.

Suddenly there was a slight movement in the brush beside Manuel, and a big mamba snake rose up before them, swaying on its tail. It hissed. Its tongue flew back and forth wickedly. Manuel crouched behind the big hunter, frozen with fear.

The hunter did not move. Was he brave, or just ignorant of mambas? Then, suddenly, Mr. Hammar shot the snake. He shot its head completely off.

"What are you scared of, boy?" Mr. Hammar sneered in disgust. "The snake is dead, you know." Then he looked around, his head cocked to one side, and he pushed the gun in Manuel's ribs again.

"I hear elephants. I'm not a fool, you know. Let's go down this way," and he pointed down the river toward the bend.

Then there came through the air the trumpeting call of the old bull elephant, loud and harsh. He had heard the shot and was calling his herd together.

As though in a nightmare, Manuel stumbled forward through the matted grass. Then he heard a familiar squeal.

"What was that?" hissed Mr. Hammar. They stopped and looked around.

Some baboons screamed from a nearby tree. They jumped from limb to limb, their black paws grabbing the branches. Then they disappeared, round pink bottoms showing through the green.

"Was it the baboons?" questioned Manuel.

Just then a young elephant cavorted out of the brush. Manuel gasped. It was his baby elephant of yesterday. Behind the little elephant lumbered the cow elephant, slowly and silently following her child.

Mr. Hammar was taken by surprise. He stood and gaped. Perhaps the size of the cow astonished him.

The baby elephant came fearlessly to Manuel and rubbed his ears against Manuel's shirt. Then he reached into Manuel's pocket with his trunk and found the peanuts Manuel had put there.

"Don't hurt him. I fed him the other day," begged Manuel.

The cow elephant stood there, watching. Her trunk was erect and her ears were widespread.

"He's too small to shoot," said the hunter. "But look at that cow. She's like a young mountain." The hunter raised his gun. Manuel gasped in horror.

At the movement of the gun, the baby elephant let out a startled squeal.

The big cow lunged forward with her trunk held high. She charged at the hunter in a huge half circle. Her ugly yellow eyes were aflame with hate. Her big ears spread wider.

Manuel crouched behind the young elephant. The baby rubbed his ears against Manuel's shoulder, and whimpered. He was frightened too.

The hunter's shot creased the wrinkled gray hide of the cow elephant. Then, CRASH! She stiffened her trunk and whammed it down on top of the hunter's head with a resounding whack. And the hunter dropped to the earth.

Then the huge cow trumpeted to her child, and, shoving him ahead of her, they went down to the river together.

Manuel climbed the tree to watch them. Far, far away, he could see the elephant herd leaving the river and disappearing into the jungle. They would be safe now.

There was a whistle below. Manuel looked down and saw Bolamba. He had discarded his clothes, and his body was covered with stripes of paint. He carried a spear. Behind him were the native boy guides. All were naked. All had spears. All were painted. They circled the hunter, crumpled on the ground, and Manuel could hear hate and anger in their mutterings.

Manuel understood now. If the hunter had shot the elephant, he would have been killed by these boys.

Manuel climbed down the tree. He was trembling, but he said stanchly,

"Bolamba, help me carry the hunter to the trading post."

Bolamba and the boys grudgingly helped carry the limp man to the jeep. They acted as if they were handling something unclean.

The native boys set off toward their village, and Bolamba rode with Manuel back to the trading post.

Carlos and Maria listened to the horrible story. Carlos examined the hunter sprawled in the back of the jeep.

"He's only knocked unconscious," said Carlos. "I will telephone for the police. They can take him to a hospital, and I will forbid him to return to this trading post. He is a trouble-maker."

The desperate hour was over. Never again would Manuel be as frightened as he had been on the bluff with the hunter and the angry elephant.

"Bolamba," Manuel was laughing with relief, "go put on some of my clothes, and I will teach you to drive forward, not backward."

Both boys shouted with laughter, to the puzzlement of Carlos and Maria.

CHAPTER 6

The Night with the Elephants

There came a rainless spell. The blessed showers did not fall, and the veldt began to turn yellow, and wither.

Manuel was invited to attend a Prayer-for-Rain dance in Bolamba's village. He drove over in the jeep, carrying the can of nuts, just in case he had an opportunity to visit the elephants.

Bolamba said he knew the elephants were still in the jungle because he heard their noises at early dawn.

After a great feast, the warriors gathered for the dance. First came the monotonous, everlasting sound of the drums. Then wild shouting and singing and chanting. The dance itself was exciting, bold and fierce.

There were circles of black men, their bodies glistening with sweat and paint. Round and round the fire they danced. Sometimes they stopped to gaze at the white stars above and cry out for rain. They shook their spears at the heavens, and stamped the earth hard with bare feet. It seemed to Manuel that the men were threatening their gods. This kept on and on until the dancers were in a frenzy, and Manuel was frightened.

Then dark scudding clouds obscured the white stars. The high moon disappeared. There was ominous thunder, and lightning cut the black sky. The wind began to blow, and suddenly a hard vertical rain fell.

Now the men were mad with joy. They stood with their painted faces held up to the rain and howled like animals. Manuel took shelter from the rain in a hut with a peaked roof. He rejoiced that the prayers of the natives had been answered, and wondered if they possessed any magic that the Portuguese did not know. He had never heard his parents praying rain down from the heavens.

The brief storm was soon over, and the natives had another feast of roast goat, python, and monkey meat. The women dragged out huge baskets of corn, roots, and sweet potatoes to add to the feast. Manuel ate until he was stuffed. It was very late when he returned to the mud hut to sleep with Bolamba under the thatched roof rustling with lizards.

Later in the night Manuel was awakened by Mjob rudely shaking his shoulder.

"Wake, Manuel! Bolamba!" whispered Mjob. "Hear the drums talk. Kosa warriors are gathering to kill the white men. A Sacred Elephant has been shot."

Manuel could hear the ominous sound of the drums, filling the jungle and the veldt. And suddenly the chief himself was in the hut.

"Friend of my son," he said, "you must return to your home quickly." Kind hands then picked Manuel up and placed him in the back of the jeep and covered him with straw.

"Bolamba," ordered the chief, "you drive this boy to the trading post, to the protection of his father."

Bolamba jumped into the driver's seat, put the jeep in gear, and drove away jerkily, with Mjob standing in the back, and Manuel crouched under the straw.

It all happened so suddenly that Manuel was breathless and frightened.

"Why are you sending me away?" he asked. "I am your friend, and I love the elephants." Manuel could hardly keep from crying because his friends trusted him so little.

"The chief and our people know that you love the elephants," replied Mjob, "but the other tribes are rising against all white people. They have trampled on our sacred customs.

Now, you stay under the straw. I go ahead to warn your father." And Mjob leaped from the jeep into the dark brush.

"How will he get there ahead of the jeep?" asked Manuel.

"Mjob knows a secret Kosa trail," replied Bolamba, turning back to look at Manuel. "Now, you keep your head down and cover your face. White faces shine in the dark."

The native boy drove surely through the forest and over the veldt. Manuel felt pride in Bolamba's driving.

The jeep rumbled along, and Manuel lay in the back, well covered with straw. On and on they jolted. Manuel peeked out and saw the stars tangled in the treetops. The rainstorm had left the air cold and damp.

Once Manuel heard monkeys, and he lifted his head in time to see an old male monkey leading his clan on a forage.

Bolamba made a sound for caution. He took his foot off the

gas and let the jeep drift silently down a slope, over the thick matted grass. The high brush fenced them in as they coasted down to the old elephant road.

Bolamba stood high on the seat and parted the grass.

"Manuel, come, look," he whispered.

Manuel arose and looked. Farther down below he could see many warriors, their faces blue-black in the white moonlight. They held high their spears and chanted a war song. Some were already painted.

"They are asking the Gods of War to bless their spears," explained Bolamba. Manuel nodded. He knew, and he chilled with fear.

"You cannot go farther," decided Bolamba. "Better to return and hide with the elephant herd."

So, as silently as possible, the boys took the old can of pea-

nuts from the jeep and trudged through the high grass, back to the bluff. They slid down its steep sides to the bank of the river below, where the elephant herd still splashed and fed and nursed their children in the night.

Bolamba picked out a giant tree with a fine thick crown.

"Climb up here and wait," he said. "If the elephants should bother you, just drop some peanuts down to them."

Manuel climbed the tree swiftly, and Bolamba tossed the can of nuts up to him. The herd had not noticed him yet, for the wind was blowing toward him. Bolamba said, "I go to tell your father. We will return." And he vanished into the dark.

Go with God, Bolamba, and may you reach the trading post safely, Manuel said silently.

He sat quietly in the great tree, listening intently for any sign of trouble from Bolamba. There were no sounds but the strange cries of the night animals and birds of the jungle.

Manuel watched the elephants down in the river. He was not afraid of the elephant herd, only of the warriors, prowling the night, seeking to kill white men.

Who could have been so cruel, so foolish, as to kill one of their Sacred Elephants?

Before long the elephant child discovered Manuel; he squealed with delight, and seemed happy to see Manuel up there in the tree, or perhaps he smelled the nuts. Manuel knew

58

that the elephant child below him was really begging, so the boy obligingly dropped down a few nuts.

That was all that was necessary to keep the elephant there. Again and again Manuel tossed nuts down to the greedy animal, while the big cow elephant stood by. When a young male showed an interest in the nuts, the old mother whacked him savagely with her trunk and sent him scurrying away.

Manuel eyed her with respect. She must be the biggest mother in the whole wide world. Her ears alone would make two dining-room tables.

Finally the can of nuts was empty; but the elephant child still begged, so Manuel threw the can to him. He caught it with delight, only to toss it into the air and run after it. What fun he had! Just like a boy playing catch. Soon the can was mashed flat, but the elephant child still threw it high and kicked it around.

Manuel settled back in the tree to wait for help and watch the herd. The old cow elephant stood beneath the tree. Whenever a curious elephant approached to look at Manuel, she charged him with ears widespread and trunk held high. She trumpeted angrily. Was she protecting Manuel because her child liked him? Manuel did not know. Mjob once said that elephants never forget a friend.

How much like people the elephants were, Manuel thought.

If the hunters only understood them, they would not be so anxious to shoot them.

A fine young bull elephant was showing off for a cow elephant. The young bull trumpeted. He cavorted around on the riverbank in a ridiculous, clumsy fashion. He even plucked leaves from a tree and offered them to his love.

At first she was indifferent or shy. Manuel didn't know which. But finally she responded to the big fellow's attentions by squealing excitedly and rubbing her flapping ears against his broad side . . . and then . . . they lifted their heads high and, with trunks entwined, actually kissed each other.

Then the cow butted her boy friend playfully, and ran off into the jungle. The male trumpeted and thundered clumsily after her.

Manuel shifted to a more comfortable position on a broad limb, with his back resting against the trunk of the tree. He wondered how far away Bolamba was now. Surely he must be at the trading post.

The elephant child returned from his game with the can. He stood beneath the tree, evidently weary. His mother fondled him with her trunk. She went to the river and returned and squirted water over the little fellow, giving him a bath. She squeaked and chirruped to him in a motherly way. But when he tried to nurse, she gave him a big wallop with her trunk and left him whining and spluttering.

Little boy, you will just have to grow up, thought Manuel. Then he had to laugh, for the young elephant plucked a branch from the tree and wiped the mosquitoes off his back. Manuel decided that he must be the smartest elephant child in the jungle.

CHAPTER 7

Go with God, Little Elephant

"Manuel." The voice of Carlos came through the treetop where Manuel was dozing. "Manuel, wake up. I'm here."

Manuel awoke with a start. It was a few minutes before he located his father and Mjob, peering down at him from the bluff.

Manuel hastily climbed down from the tree. He gave the elephant child an affectionate pat, and climbed up the bluff on hands and knees, to get to his father as quickly as possible.

The baby elephant tried to follow, but the way was too steep, and he slid backward. The disappointed baby bellowed after Manuel, and caused his mother to come over and chirrup fondly to comfort him.

"I'm sure glad to see you," gasped Manuel. "What took you so long?"

"We have bad news, son," answered Carlos. "Bolamba was struck in the back with a spear while driving the jeep. The spear was probably meant for you. Maria is caring for him. Come, we must hurry."

Manuel was stunned. Bolamba, his best friend, struck by a spear meant for him. Oh, why did he ever teach him to drive?

Manuel cried as he stumbled after his father and Mjob to where the jeep was parked.

"You must return alone to the trading post," said Mjob. "I will go to my father and tell him the evil thing the warriors have done."

"Mjob," said Carlos earnestly, "tell your father that we will not flee to Johannesburg now. We will remain and nurse Bolamba. He is very dear to us."

Tears seemed to glisten on Mjob's blue-black face, but he said nothing. He disappeared in the brush, and Manuel climbed into the jeep after his father.

The jeep lurched through the night back to the trading post. The monotonous drums sounded through the dark. War drums. Manuel forgot to be afraid. He thought only of his friend, and his throat ached with suppressed sobs.

When they reached the trading post, Maria had a light in every window. She was alone with the boy.

"How is he?" Carlos asked tersely.

"He is sleeping. I removed the spear and cleaned the wound," replied Maria.

"Did you give him something to relieve the pain?" asked Carlos.

"Yes, and some penicillin, too," Maria told him. "His pulse is weak from loss of blood. I hope the spear was not poisoned."

"We'll find out if it was poisoned when the chief comes," Carlos said.

Manuel sat in the corner, out of the way, and watched his parents nursing Bolamba. Manuel felt as though this were his fault. He should have been driving the jeep, not his friend, Bolamba. The wounded boy's face was twisted with pain, and now and then he moaned.

Suddenly the distant drums were silent.

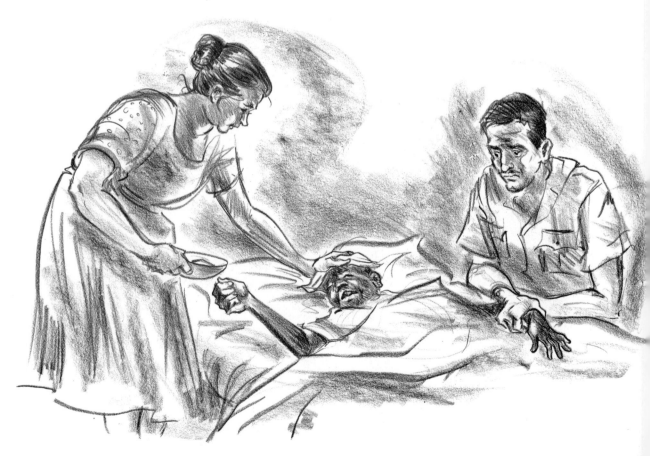

"The chief has received the news," Manuel said.

Carlos nodded his head in agreement.

"Yes," he said. "The jungle war is over for a time."

Carlos was right. The incessant animal calls from the jungle resumed, and night birds sang. Before long the chief himself appeared, followed by his medicine man, his wives, and most of his tribe.

The chief was in an agony of grief. His medicine man, his wives, and braves all squatted silently outside the house.

"Carlos," said the chief, approaching the boy's cot, "use white man's medicine. Use black man's medicine. My son must not die."

"Chief," said Carlos, "was the spear poisoned?"

"Let me see spear," replied the chief. "Old warriors use poisoned spears. Young warriors do not."

Maria brought out the spear, and the chief examined it.

"Yes, it was poisoned," he determined. "Tika!" the chief shouted to the medicine man. "Bring herbs to fight poison of spear."

"Thank God they have an antidote," Maria murmured.

Manuel watched intently. Perhaps the medicine man could help save Bolamba. Tika brought out some dried leaves from a pouch he carried. The leaves appeared to be like holly leaves.

Tika built a fire in the yard, heated some water in a tin can, and, when the water was boiling, dropped in the dried leaves. He stirred the mixture with a stick, and brewed a dark-colored tea.

"Give this to boy to drink," Tika instructed Maria.

"Do as he says," Carlos told her when she hesitated. "It's their antidote for the poison."

Maria cooled the dark tea by blowing on it, and then coaxed Bolamba to awaken. She held his head up and fed the mixture to him, a spoonful at a time, until it was all gone.

Bolamba lay down and went into a deep sleep. Perspiration rolled from his face, yet he seemed to shiver.

Maria sat by the shivering boy and held the blankets around him. Outside, Tika chanted prayers to his tribal gods. He danced around the fire, and now the solemn, quiet people squatting outside joined in the chants.

Manuel drew nearer to watch. Tika produced cakes from his pouch, made of fried gnats, and offered them to his gods by burning them in the fire. Then he took out an old cigar box full of dead spiders and reptiles' tails, which he threw in the fire.

The chief paced up and down by Bolamba's cot, watching every breath of the boy.

Outside, more and more black men gathered. Now the women wailed and wept, as they swayed back and forth on

the ground. Manuel realized that they were not angry with the white people now. The whole tribe had forgotten their anger. They were profoundly touched by the suffering of the crumpled boy on the cot. They felt a terrible sorrow for the evil thing they had done—throwing a spear into the back of the son of the chief.

"They thought I was driving," Manuel muttered to himself. He shuddered. Yet he was as innocent as Bolamba of shooting an elephant.

It was a long night for Manuel, listening to the labored breathing of Bolamba, and praying for his recovery.

Toward dawn the warrior who threw the fatal spear was discovered. He was dragged before the chief, a cringing old man, tattooed and scarred with many battle wounds.

The old warrior knelt in the dirt and begged for mercy.

"Tie him on the anthill," roared the chief, his voice filled with hate.

The natives dragged the culprit outside the trading post and tied him to stakes in the big anthill where Bolamba had learned to drive. When the ants came out in the morning, they would gradually eat the man alive.

Manuel ran inside to his father. "Father," he whispered, "they have tied an old man to the large anthill. He is the one who threw the spear. Father, the ants will kill him. What can we do?"

Carlos left the bedside of Bolamba, and walked directly to the chief, where he paced back and forth, now chanting prayers with his tribe.

"Chief," said Carlos firmly, "you must make a sacrifice if you want your son to live."

"Yes, yes," agreed the chief gladly. "Tell me what sacrifice. Anything you say I will do."

"You must give up the pleasure of revenge. You must let the old warrior go free." Carlos spoke out with all the authority he could muster.

"Oh," grunted the chief. He was taken aback by the order of Carlos.

He hesitated only a moment; then he agreed.

"Let the man go free," ordered the chief, "but tell him he must never carry a spear again. He shall live as a woman for the rest of his days, tending the cooking pots and the children. I have spoken."

Maria gave Bolamba another penicillin powder, and together the family watched by his cot. The crowd outside milled around, now chanting and wailing.

The guilty old man was kept busy working with the women, feeding the warriors; but he bore his shame well, being always careful to keep out of the chief's way.

Word came the next day that the forestry officials had arrested the hunters who had shot the Sacred Elephant, and deported them from the country. They were forever banished from Mozambique.

Then word came by messenger that the wounded elephant had not died. He had risen from the ground and disappeared into the jungle. The natives rejoiced at this news.

But although all of these things were important, the labored breathing of the boy on the cot was more important. The tattooed warriors came again and again to the door to stare at Bolamba, sorrow in their dark eyes.

Bolamba's suffering had touched the tenderness underneath the natives' cruel, bold front. Each in his own way watched and prayed at the cot of the stricken son of their chief.

On the third day Bolamba was better, and all rejoiced. Then it was that Mjob whispered to Manuel, "Come, drive me in your jeep to the elephant herd. I want to show you something wonderful that is happening."

The two boys slipped away unnoticed.

High on the bluff they looked down on the elephant herd. The elephants had been by the river so long now that the bank looked like a battlefield. Trees were uprooted. The grass was all eaten. The soil was trampled smooth and hard. There was mud on the tree trunks where the elephants had rubbed themselves. White egrets were everywhere.

Manuel saw four immense elephants in the distance. They were approaching the river.

"Look carefully," said Mjob. "See what they are doing."

Manuel looked carefully. They were very large, as large as four great mountains. He had never seen such huge elephants. What were they doing, all huddled together like that? And then he could see. Who would believe it? They were helping a fifth elephant, who was apparently wounded. As they drew near, Manuel could see where the blood and gore had run down the folded gray side of the elephant.

"That must be the Sacred Elephant the hunters shot! See! He did not die!" Mjob spoke with great gladness in his voice.

The four huge elephants were using their strong dark serpent-like trunks to support the wounded elephant. They reached under his belly and actually carried him along with their trunks. They all stopped often to rest. Once they hosed the wounded elephant with water from the river. Then they pulled up great swaths of grass and offered it to him to eat.

"Elephants always take care of their own," Mjob told Manuel.

Manuel and Mjob watched until the strange rescue party disappeared into the dark jungle, with their wounded comrade struggling along between them.

The two boys reluctantly returned to the trading post.

Bolamba was definitely better. He sat up on the cot and ate sliced bananas with cream and sugar, given him by Maria; and he also ate slices of dried python meat, given him by the medicine man, Tika.

"Yah! Yah!" shouted the chief to everyone. "My son will recover. The black man's medicine is good. The white man's medicine is good!" Then he gave an order to his wives that Manuel could not understand, and they ran out into the veldt.

Manuel wondered where the women were going, but he was in such a hurry to tell Bolamba about the Sacred Elephants helping their wounded comrade that he didn't bother to ask.

"I am glad the Sacred Elephant didn't die," said Bolamba when he heard the story. "Oh, I wish I had seen them helping him."

"Bolamba, you should have seen how tenderly the big strong ones cared for the wounded one," Manuel said. "You really missed a wonderful sight. I think your Sacred Elephants must be the strongest elephants in all Africa, to lift another elephant right off the ground like that. And they are so intelligent, to figure out how to do it! Why, I'll wager they have as much sense as a man has."

The boys talked for a long time. They were glad to be together again.

74

"I felt awful when they told me you were struck by the spear meant for me," Manuel told his friend.

"It was all a mistake," said Bolamba. "Father says they will wait for the police to act, if another elephant is ever shot."

"I'm sure that no one will ever shoot another one," said Manuel. "This was published in all the papers and broadcast over the radio. People must know now that they cannot shoot Sacred Elephants."

Then Manuel heard a loud clamor. The women were returning, leading many goats on tethers. And right there, outside the trading post, the women proceeded to prepare another feast of roast goat. This was the chief's way of honoring the Lopez family for nursing Bolamba back to health.

While they were feasting that night, from far away in the jungle came an insistent trumpeting.

"What is that?" asked Maria.

"The Sacred Elephants are leaving," replied Mjob.

Manuel walked to the edge of the clearing and looked out. The distant bluff, where they had observed the elephants, was a brown smudge in the night sky. The veldt stretched far ahead of him. He could hear nearby frogs croaking, like rusty hinges; and the cicadas singing. But above these close sounds came the urgent trumpeting of the bull elephant.

76

The Sacred Elephants were leaving. He did not know when they would return, if ever. Perhaps he would never see the elephant child again, his wonderful elephant child.

"Go with God, little elephant," Manuel whispered into the night.